The World I Want to See

Devajit Bhuyan

Ukiyoto Publishing

All global publishing rights are held by

Ukiyoto Publishing

Published in 2023

Content Copyright © Devajit Bhuyan

ISBN 9789360168728

All rights reserved.
No part of this publication may be reproduced,
transmitted, or stored in a retrieval system, in any
form by any means, electronic, mechanical,
photocopying, recording or otherwise, without the
prior permission of the publisher.

The moral rights of the author have been asserted.

This book is sold subject to the condition that it shall
not by way of trade or otherwise, be lent, resold, hired
out or otherwise circulated, without the publisher's
prior consent, in any form of binding or cover other
than that in which it is published.

www.ukiyoto.com

Dedicated to my beloved wife late
Mitali Bhuyan

The World I Want to See
The World I Want to See
The World I Want to See

"She was part of a group that helped tilt the world just a tiny bit the right way. Yes, she one tiny person, was part of it. Hardly noticeable, true, but 'hardly' was more than nothing. 'Hardly' made all the difference in the world in how she saw herself."

Ray Smith, The Magnolia That Bloomed Unseen

Dedicated to my beloved wife late Mitali Bhuyan, who tried to make the world a better place for everyone.

Contents

The World I Want To See	1
Beginning Of Life	2
Life Without Intoxication	3
Divided World	4
Labour Pain	5
Grass On The Other Side	6
Move Forward	7
Winning Profile	8
Three Problems	9
If And But	10
Journey Is The Award	11
Greed And Need	12
A Salt With Sodium	13
God Is Without Need	14
Death	15
Brotherhood	16
Bubble	17
Uncertainty Is Beauty	18
Let Us Live Like Brother	19
Give Peace A Chance	20
Life's Journey	21
Patriotism	22
Nationalism	23

Nation First	24
What Civilization Is Not	25
Climate	26
Climate Change	27
Nobody Wants War	28
Crash	29
Crawl	30
Craze	31
Time	32
Time Is Fine	33
Computer Virus	34
Court	35
Courtesy Light	36
Appreciate When One Is Alive	37
Cape Town Water Crisis	38
Cover	39
Rain Remove Dust	40
Cow	41
The Game Of Uncertainty	42
Loneliness	43
Bank Balance	44
When You Are In Traffic Jam	45
Sinusoidal Cricket	46
Corruption	47
Crab	48
Crack	49

Hobby And Profession	50
Flood	51
Cream	52
Sos	53
Nudity	54
Credit	55
Copyright	56
Crisis	57
Credential	58
Bedtime Poem	59
Critic	60
Criticise	61
Culture	62
The Dog	63
Cunning	64
Current	65
Money Has Relative Value	66
Cynic	67
Alcohol	68
Tree And Me	69
The Ladder Of Death	71
Say Goodbye!	72
Beauty Is Everywhere	73
British, The Exploiter	74
Love And Death	76
The Holes	77

Are We Witnessing Trailers?	78
An Outdated Soul	79
Man Proposes, God Disposes!	80
Life Is A Tragic Play	81
Enjoy Silence For A Day Or Two	82
Don't Pray For Gain	83
Don't Wait, Make Your Bust Today	84
Strong Man Doesn't Cry	85
Love Is Not In The Hand Of God Now	86
Infidelity	87
Shiva The Destroyer	88
Health Alone Is Not Wealth	89
Climbing Everest Is Easy	90
Widows Of Vrindavana (Brindaban)	91
Christ	92
He Sacrificed Life	93
Cross	94
Christmas	95
Church	96
He Made This	97
My God Died Young	98
Buddhism	99
Messenger Of Peace	100
Dalai Lama	101
Traveling	102
Daddy	103

Dance	104
Danger	105
Past	106
Caste System	107
Benchmark	108
Bipolar World	109
Black And White	110
Black Hole	111
Do A Memorable Job Today	112
Climate Change Is Disturbing	113
So Insignificant We Are	114
Reasons Many	115
Mistake	116
Our Existence	117
God And Nothing Of Physics	118
Inquisitiveness	119
Not Everything Matters Of Science	120
Purpose Of Life	121
Purpose Of Life-2	122
Blame Game	123
Blessing	124
Blotting Paper	125
Bluetooth	126
Boat	127
Anger	128
If You Are Right	129

Body Language	130
You Are Bold	131
Bonus	132
Booby Trap	133
Brainstorm	134
Bribe	135
Brain Drain	136
Bridge	137
Brief	138
Bull	139
Buoyant	140
No One Is Indispensable	141
Atom	142
Café	143
Cadet	144
Butterfly	145
Butterfly Chasing	146
Cake	147
Calendar	148
Call Centre	149
Camel	150
Camera	151
Cancer	152
Candle	153
Candy	154
Canvas	155

Cap	156
Capability	157
Capital	158
Captain	159
Caption	160
Carbon	161
Environment	162
Let The Tears Flow	163
Centre Of Life	164
Contraceptive	165
Condom	166
Control	167
Convert	168
Convenience	169
Conviction	170
Cooperate	171
Cook	172
Coordination	173
Copper	174
Companion	175
Copycat	176
Morning Shows The Day	177
Failure	178
Critics Will Never Appreciate	179
Correspondent	180
Corrupt	181

Jungle	182
My Inconsistent Mind	183
Proud	184
We Are Actor	185
Religion	186
Religion And Politics	187
Zoom	188
I Want To Be A Kid	189
Father's Day	190
Yacht	191
Yoga	192
Today Is Best Day To Feel Happy	193
Gratitude	194
Cost	195
Count	196
Best Policy Of Living	197
Sun Will Rise Soon	198
Single	199
Birthday	200
Counter	201
Country	202
Sacrifice	203
Walk	204
Water	205
Umbrella	206
Coma	207

Zebra	208
Zeal	209
Comfort	210
Comedy	211
Zero	212
Commando	213
Commentator	214
Citizen, Please Remember	215
Alcohol	216
Class	217
Clean	218
Clap	219
Deep Corner Of Heart	220
Move On	221
The Show Must Go On	222
Worst Cruelty	223
Counting	224
Enjoy With Smile	225
Citizen	226
Cigarette	227
Cinderella	228
Cinema	229
Circle	230
Tell Me Your Companion	231
Indian Parents	232
Chromosome	233

Time Heal Time Kill	234
One Night's Guest	235
Chloroform	236
Chlorophyll	237
Beautiful Today	238
Final Corollary	239
When Jesus In Heart	240
Continent	241
Longevity Is Not The Yardstick	242
Today Is Mine	243
Confidence	244
About the Author	*245*

The World I Want To See

I want to see a world free from hate
With cruelty no one wish to date
The world is with zero crime rate
Future of child is not determined by fate
Honesty is every human's soul mate;
I want to see a world free from violence
Everyone follow the path of tolerance
No one dies of hunger and war
Gender inequality doesn't create scar
Human values shine like bright star;
I want to see a world free from caste
Humanity is the only religion everyone trust
Boundaries of nation diminished forever
Mind is without fear to rise tall and higher
Society will strive with intellectual desire;
I want to see a world free from greed
For environment and ecology everyone heed
Protecting biodiversity every individual lead
Man animal conflict not known to any kid
In outer space human foot print technology will seed.

Beginning Of Life

Love making is divine, it is the beginning of motherhood

New life breeds in the union of two independent bodies

Souls cannot be created without coming together physically

So, every soul, higher or lower order, bounded bodily

And in existence, bodies suffer physically and souls mentally

When we term sex as dirty, we disrespect motherhood

Without motherhood, there cannot be any brotherhood

Life is beyond basic needs of food, clothes and shelter

Mother is the fulcrum of all the social relationships

Without mother, natural or adopted, life is incomplete

Within mother, love, God, and relationships exists.

Life Without Intoxication

Life itself is interesting and intoxicating
No other intoxication is necessary
Drugs and alcohol always destroy health
Gambling can destroy heard earned wealth
If you can't live without intoxication, what is living?
Outside alcohol you can't make life interesting
Some people say intoxication helps creativity
But in family and social life it also makes cavity
Let your heart and mind see the world without simulation
To win a Olympic medal, drugs is not a good solution
You can be stripped at any point in doping test
Journey of life without drugs, alcohol and gambling is best.

Divided World

This is a divided world
Will never come to one fold
Divided in the name of religion
Divided in the name of region
Divided in the name of country
Divided in the name of boundary
Divided in the name of caste and creed
Divided in the name of colour and breed
We the human planted dividing seed
We the human distribute divisive feed
Nature gave us diversity for balance
By destroying it our existence we challenge.

Labour Pain

Mothers only know the intensity of labour pain

May be the newborn cry, seeing mom's suffering

Hearing the cry of the child she forgets everything

Her focus is only the newborn baby's well-being

The arms and lap of the mother is newborn's comfort zone

The newborn realize that s/he is safe and no can do harm

The tigress with new calf is dangerous is well known

Even mother a small animal will fight till death to save the kid

Everything the mother will do to keep newborn safe and feed

Sacrifice is the basic instinct of motherhood

Her goal is to make her newborn self-sufficient and good

That is why mother is unique creation of nature and God

The wheels of Civilization motherhood only unfold.

Grass On The Other Side

Sometimes the grass on the other side is really green

This is the reason why migration takes place

Without nomadic life, the civilization would have been static

Hope of greener grass was migrations real motive

Even now, now software engineers are not static

People still migrate to another country leaving all

Because they see the grasses on other side is green and tall

They leave culture, language and even religion for better life

But in the world of survival of fittest, for some it remain as hype

Success and good quality of life is possible everywhere

Without potential and hard work, even in America, you may be nowhere.

Move Forward

Cloud can't shadow sun for long
After the rain sun is back and strong
Even a wind can chase away cloud
Along with sun ray rainbow is found;
Hurdles are only to test your endurance
During difficult period show your prudence
Soon problems will fly away with time
Critics will become speechless and mime;
After Sunset morning comes always
Full moon pushes darkness by silvery rays
Don't be afraid of temporary setback
Move forward, good days will come back.

Winning Profile

Never live life with inferiority complex
Make your life beautiful and duplex
No need to live hiding your face
Like a powerful horse join the race
No need to bow your head even you lose
Fighting back attitude you must choose
Move forward galloping with a smile
To reach goal you have to go thousands mile
With inferiority complex don't be fragile
Confidence, attitude your winning profile.

Three Problems

Basic root of all problems is money
Yet in this world money is the best honey
It can make or break life's long journey;
Relationships are always problem major
Many a time in life it can bring horror
Money can lighten relationship corridor;
Health problems can make or break life
Money can give good health is only hype
Through incurable disease richest can wipe;
Take care of money, relation and health
Relationships and health better wealth
Fine balancing give happiness till death.

If And But

Don't waste time on if and but
Rather sharpen edge for the cut
If and but are words for post-mortem
Critics used it to criticise and condemn
If and but are only for correcting course
For if and but don't stop galloping horse
Analyse all options before you start
Once started stick to the moment last.

Journey Is The Award

Life is a journey not destination
Enjoy every moment with satisfaction
Similar things may come in rotation
But it will be always in different orientation
The journey is pain and pleasures combination;
Look to the station you have crossed
Forever it's beauty will vanish and lost
Only memory will remain till the end
So with smile gather many, many friend
Remember in the end journey is the award.

Greed And Need

Man has unlimited greed
Animals satisfied with need
Food, cloth, shelter man never agreed
All other living beings happy with feed
Thought, greed made man animal in lead;
Greed is good as long as it is motivating
If it becomes everything it is subverting
Never make greed companion everlasting
Throwing away greed will make soul's lighting
You can get rid of unwanted materialistic fighting.

A Salt With Sodium

Religion is like opium
A salt with sodium
But never dissolve like barium
Priest sale it for premium;
Religion is necessary evil
It only created the devil
Good teaching people forget
Misusing religion never regret;
No religion say become corrupt
For greed people change abrupt
Easily do violence and offence
Used religion for self-defence;
Religion failed to change people
Adam, Eve always greedy for apple
No one follow Jesus's path simple
So the society now a days horrible.

God Is Without Need

God created man
Man created him
So no one has seen
His existence is thin
To pray God all are keen;
God created man
Man created religion
He never gave permission
God went to oblivion
He is in unknown dimension;
God created man
Caste creed man's selfish greed
Gender inequality not God's seed
Man planned divisive breed
God is omnipotent without need.

Death

The opposite of life is death
Immortality is only a myth
No one can live forever
Death warrant always there
For death no need to fear;
Death is always uncertain
Any moment may fall curtain
With death no one bargain
Good health always maintain;
Death is ultimate truth in life
You ashes will flow through pipe
Enjoy and love before death come
Time will not return once it is gone.

Brotherhood

Brotherhood is missing in every corner
Society is so becoming hot burner
For brotherhood every one need runner
No one is interested to become Turner
Every child must be a brotherhood learner
Family, state, nation all needs brotherhood
Development does not mean only food
Only on brotherhood prosperity can stood
Brotherhood is missing in same religion
In family instead of brotherhood rebellion
For brotherhood let us create social opinion.

Bubble

Our life is like a bubble
For existence struggle
Bubble is always transparent
So, acquire same temperament
Transparency gives bubble rainbow
In life transparency open new window
Bubbles fly with joy towards the sky
But showing rainbow burst saying goodbye
Death may call us any moment
So, enjoy the life's beautiful tournament.

Uncertainty Is Beauty

Uncertainty is the core of life
Longevity is only hope and hype
You may die before you ripe
Beauty of life is its uncertainty
Why spoil life working for longevity
Smile and enjoy the present moment
Don't bother for your doctor's comment
Dine, wine and dance in the beach
Despite uncertainty make today rich
Death may come without any warning
No one can claim I will see next morning.

Let Us Live Like Brother

Why this madness for blood
Why play with innocent life
For whom these killings
What stopped us for brotherhood?
O' thy common people of Pakistan
Once if you understand Hindustan
You will overthrow the cruel leader
In your country there is not enough fodder
No need of a inhuman destructive war
Nothing will be gained fighting with neighbour
Give up violence let us live like brother.

Give Peace A Chance

War will lead to destruction
Peace will bring construction
War will give economy frustration
People have to live in starvation
Millions of people are still homeless
Malnutrition children are countless
Inflation will make poor people penniless
Innocent children will die for nothing
Peace can only give us better thing
Don't play the drum of painful battle
Leaders, through discussion please settle.

Life's Journey

Life is not a fairy-tale journey
Nor it is a one-day tourney
Life is indefinite hurdle race
Difficulty every moment to face
The road may not be smooth
The environment may be ruth
Jump the hurdle and move forward
In between accept cheers and reward
Even if you fell down stand up again
Don't wait though there is heavy rain
Move on move on till the final destination
Your journey is your life's real remuneration.

Patriotism

Patriotism is not delicious meal
Patriotism is a matter to feel
Patriotism give citizens zeal
Patriotism is for unity deal
Patriotism is not for divide and kill
Patriotism is for integrity heal
Patriotism is not for peel
Patriotism also inspires reel
Patriotism is attitude to chill.

Nationalism

When country is below religion
Nation saw its many division
Religion is a destructive force now
Nobody knows it can be controlled how?
Religion is part and parcel of society
But it has failed to infuse integrity
Islamic nations are fighting within
War is Arab world's daily routine
Nationalism must grow above religion
Third world countries will improve position.

Nation First

Nation first
Unity must
India vast
Attitude cast
Division rust
Grow trust
Throw lust
History past
Enemy dust
Religion last
Nation first.

What Civilization Is Not

War is not civilization

It brings only destruction

Ashoka is not great for war

He propagated peace too far

Bin Laden is not civilization

Mother Teresa is justification

Hiroshima bombing not civilization

It reminds devastating destruction

Civilization is Japan's new constitution.

Climate

The four seasons make climate
For survival of animals, it is ultimate
Sunshine, rain, humidity, cold weather
All makes climate of a place together
Climate determines vegetation and tree
In the ever-green forest animal live free
Climate is the factor for biodiversity
Don't destroy climate for modernity.

Climate Change

The biggest threat to mankind

We must stop climate unwind

It is very difficult to rewind

Solution to change must be find

Climate change can destroy civilization

Climate change is not for standardization

Biodiversity and climate complex combination

Many species will face extinction

To stop climate change society need determination.

Nobody Wants War

Nobody wants war
It pushes back far
Life becomes coal tar
Think ways how to bar
Terrorism is evil
War is also devil
People war will kill
No war in revenge zeal
It will take long to heal
Yet for self-defence must fight
Self-defence is our birth right
To save own life we must put might
If we win then future will be bright.

Crash

Don't drive fast you may crash
One mistake can spoil your dress
Slow and steady can enjoy air fresh
What is the joy and fun in driving rash?
Some innocent pedestrian you may thrash
You will land in police net and legal mesh
A crash can drain in hospital all your cash
In cremation ground you may become ash;
When computer crash you lose data all
In case of airplane crash it is free fall
No one you will be able to make a call
Life is precious don't hit everywhere like ball.\

Crawl

To crawl is the nature of a child
Many animals crawl in the wild
By crawling cross the slippery field
Through in crawling progress is mild
Better satisfaction one can yield;
While running fast you may get derailed
In the rat race of success you can be failed
Through crawling always remain sailed
In the long run defeat will be unveiled
Your struggle and success one day will be hailed.

Craze

Short lived enthusiasm for something
Crazy people are busy for nothing
Stadium is full because of football craze
Some crazy supporters always amaze;
Craze can sometimes help to achieve tall
Crazy people's dreams mostly fall
Yet craze is intoxicating inspiration
Crazy scientist can find big solution.

Time

Never say time is cruel
Since beginning It is equal
Time is the communist real
Second, minute same for all
For misuse some people fall
Using better some become tall
For time no one is big or small
Work only gives fame and hall
To everyone time give call
Don't wait when on your leg ball
Hit it to score your life's goal.

Time Is Fine

Time is always fine
Utilization is only mine
As per wish I can dine
Any time I can drink wine
As per time sun shine;
Time I can always misuse
But it can never be reuse
Every moment it blow fuse
Light year is very huge
Wasting time why amuse?
Einstein got same hours in a day
Time comes to all in equal ray
But it takes own nonstop way
To nobody anything it will say
Will not give a extra even if you pay;
Time is free resource like light
Utilize time to make future bright
Abuse of time is not right
In future you will face plight
You can't do anything with your might.

Computer Virus

Virus, virus no one nowadays serious
Youngsters are only very curious
It is an unwanted software spurious
Yet for many systems virus is dangerous
For many paying for antivirus is luxurious
When computer crashes, we become furious
Virus prevention is expenses miscellaneous
The creation of virus is sadistically ceremonious.

Court

The Temple built to give justice
But now layers do their practice
Litigants run from pillar to post
Clever layers make them to roast
The people in court are bad host;
In the temple angel of justice is blind
Helpful Advocate difficult to find
Only money can make them shine
Hearing date reached one to nine
For justice pending litigation is not fine.

Courtesy Light

Make your attitude like courtesy light
Life's journey will be beautiful and bright
Sometimes friends many not be right
Yet never start an unnecessary fight
Your courtesy can save it becoming tight;
When bell rings open the door with a smile
It will make to come down the visitor hostile
When you offer a cup of tea to your critique
In future for you he will have better attic
The effects of Thank You never remain static.

Appreciate When One Is Alive

What I will gain if you remember me
After death I will be with omnipotent he
During life never saw your smiling face
Now you are smiling in the funeral race
I was tired to make you understand my case
But your thinking and vision was always haze;
No need to pray for me after final journey
I have already finished my eventful tourney
Mourning will now not change the game
After death what I will do with name and fame
During life time your habit was only to blame
With your appreciation I would not have died lame.

Cape Town Water Crisis

Not just combination of hydrogen-oxygen
It is the life line of living beings and citizen
Without water life can't continue in earth
Every moment thousands new lives birth
Ground water in cities going down and down
No new water source yet city residents found
The potable water crisis is coming around
If water is not conserved fall of cities is bound
Cape town water crisis raising alarm for many city
To resolve potable water crisis together every ones duty.

Cover

In order to protect or conceal something
Cover never represent everything
In books front and back cover is identity
Sometimes cover protect the integrity
Undercover cops fight with criminals
Vegetation used as cover by animals
Cover is necessary for aesthetic also
For some cover has to represent solo
Because inside everything are hollow.

Rain Remove Dust

When I saw your photo first
I thought one day we meet must
Our friendship doesn't gather rust
As friends we must have trust
The domain of time is very vast
In the world forever we will not last
Our relationship must be true and just
One day I will make our memorable bust
History will remember us friends of past
The rain will always remove the dust
Friendship in the world is rainbow cast.

Cow

Fully grown domesticated female animal
Without milk difficult will be kids survival
Most useful animal since time immemorial
Worshipping cow in India is traditional
Butter, cream, ghee, curd part of our food
All cow milk products are tasty and good
Beef is a high protein food in cold countries
In agricultural life cow had no boundaries
Cowboy is important part of all societies.

The Game Of Uncertainty

The glorious game of uncertainty
That is why glamour cricketing fraternity
The best team can't claim sure victory
Sometimes weakest team has better trajectory
The ball may take unexpected turn
The good player may make zero run
So for spectators' cricket is exciting fun
For bookies and gamblers it is second to none.

Loneliness

Loneliness is not solitary imprisonment
Nor loneliness is forcible punishment
Loneliness is opportunity for introspection
Thinking alone can give determination
Far from the madding crowd we get solution;
Loneliness is creation of one's own mind
Companion and friends one has to find
One become lonely when mind is blind
To others always be helpful and kind
Loneliness of soul forever will wind .

Bank Balance

When bank balance is in million
You have lot of cheerful companion
For you everyone gives good opinion
In the friends circle you are champion;
When bank balance become zero
For friends you are no more a hero
Best friends will say come tomorrow
On cheerful faces you will see sorrow;
Bank balance is nectar of our beautiful life
With good bank balance enjoyment strive
During bad days bank balance come handy
Without bank balance you not remain dandy.

When You Are In Traffic Jam

When you are in traffic jam
Don't lose your patience and calm
Rub your two hands palm
See the surroundings charm
Overtaking will do more harm
On your line remain firm
Smile to others with warm
Jam will not remain infinite term
No benefit in twisting arm
Look forward but remain mum.

Sinusoidal Cricket

A roller coaster grand finale
Up down like sinusoidal wave
Colour of cheers changed
Every now and then with every delivery
Though the field was not slippery
Millions of supporters speechless
Thousands adopt temporary blindness
Heart beats increased with every bounce
Every boundary produce cheerful sounds
Nail biting finish beyond expectation
England-Kiwi pushed cricket to perfection.

Corruption

Never indulge in corruption
It will spoil your reputation
Your integrity will be under suspicion
Life will take a negative direction
Your face value will see dilution
In society you may face humiliation
Corruption is the worst intention of mind
Everywhere corrupt people we always find
Yet toward corruption people are blind
To honest people society should be kind.

Crab

With five pairs of legs an unique animal
A tasty food like fish loved by many people
But to cook delicious crab is not simple
A heard of crabs can't move upward
Each one pulls others legs backward
Crabs are seen in various colours and sizes
Avoid crab mentality people to win prizes
Crab Temple is not for worshipping crab
It is a place to fill tummy as much as you can grab.

Crack

Crack can easily appear on your sole
But crack of mind break as a whole
In breaking of large stone crack has role
Even in big hills crack can create hole
People give up hope when crack is in soul;
Crack is necessary to break and make
Many things only crackdown can shake
Thousands of cracks earthquake can make
Crack on the earth surface even create lake
People with cracking mentality are always fake.

Hobby And Profession

For satisfying life always pursue hobby
If necessary make your own lobby
Life's journey will never become shabby
You can easily win the game of rugby
One day critics will say you hello baby;
When hobby is livelihood and profession
Doing job will give lot of satisfaction
You will not feel bored doing in succession
In your job you can achieve perfection
As an expert you will earn good reputation.

Flood

When rivers overflow uncontrolled
Water becomes hostile and bold,
Power of water increases many fold
The force of water embankment can't hold,
About destruction stories are told
Even in summer flood brings cold,
At exorbitant price vegetables are sold
History of flood destruction is very old,
Politicians, contractors earn gold
Misery of poor man remain untold.

Cream

Thick white fatty liquid on top of milk
The colour and softness is like silk
The taste of ice cream loved by all
Face cream make female beautiful doll
In society creamy layer is always tall;
Cream cracker, cream cheese nice to eat
Cream puffs taste no one can beat
With ice cream children should be treat
Butter, ghee made from cream are great
All creamy products melt when put heat.

Sos

Switch off something, switch off something
Never waste electricity for nothing,
Production of electricity is costly
Electricity damage environment slowly,
Switch off something silently
Help in protecting environment boldly,
Global warming is now warning politely
After some years it will express violently,
When we reduce in electricity consumption
We are helping environment protection.

Nudity

Nudity is life's inseparable part
Artists can express it as an art,
We born in the world without cloth
Male female union in necked is truth,
Every day we become necked for bath
Nudity is always in our life's path ,
Life can't flow without nudity
Love, sex and nudity are in solidarity.

Credit

Credit is obtained based on trust
Future payment should be must
For non-payment rating will rust
In default credit card always burst
In future you will get credit last;
Credit card stimulates expenses
Banks give you necessary services
Banks profit increases many fold
Your bank balance go down you are told
To recover unpaid property can be sold.

Copyright

Thank God no copyright on fire
Without paying royalty you can hire,
On wheel no one claimed copyright
So communication progressed bright,
Air, water, soil all are copyright free
That is why we can see lot of tree,
Copyright bad for spreading of knowledge
Bible is free, everyone can acknowledge,
Copyright caged freedom of free flow
In the world only few people can glow.

Crisis

Time of intense difficulty or danger
Don't be panic, face it all together,
Never allow crisis to cripple your attitude
Overcoming crisis will widen your latitude,
Crisis can make or break your future
Life's course may change forever
Face it with courage and confidence
Crisis will go away like a small incidence;
Use crisis to improve problem solving skill
Once you master, crisis can never kill
For perfection you need regular drill
Crisis will never come to you as bitter pill.

Credential

Utilise your inner potential
Develop your credential,
Credential indicates suitability
Your talent will get publicity,
For marketing credential must
Without credential best product rust,
When you earn credential people trust
Your success in society will be must,
Credential is accumulation from past
To become leader make credential vast.

Bedtime Poem

Plying soft ball in small court
No ace, no race, no double fault,
No service break and losing match
You can drop any number of catch,
Intention to score goal very slow
Game will be over if water flow
Better hit the target mildly and low,
No problem of ball tampering
Both players can do hammering,
You can hug your opponent boldly
Kiss everywhere as you like slowly,
At midnight when game is over
Players sleep comfortably under cover.

Critic

Critic is a person who see everything wrong
Whenever he moves he will make a dong,
Critic never found anything good or right
For silly mistakes he will start a fight,
Through his black glasses nothing is bright
Even in mid noon he never see sun light,
Majority of critics enjoy others leg pulling
In every opportunity they try to bullying,
Yet critics are necessary to identify fault
Sometimes accept them with pinch of salt.

Criticise

To criticise is the easiest thing in the world
For small mistake no one should be scold
With politeness deficiency can be told
Respect for your will always remain bold
Your courtesy will be repeatedly told;
When you criticise others on flimsy ground
Everywhere only enemy you will found
No one will lift when you fall on ground
Your harsh words will always rebound
Nobody will listen your crying sound;
Criticism is good as long as it help other
Your criticism should be like words of father
Instead of leg pulling stop your mouth rather
Go inside the situation considering self later
You will find an opinion for comment better.

Culture

Manifestation of human intellect collectively
Culture is based on climate predominantly;
Food, agriculture, vegetation influence culture
Some people offer their dead body to vulture;
Culture become integral part of lifestyle
Religion gave many culture horrible style,
Culture represents inner value of people
In world many ethnic cultures are simple,
Integration of cultures made world beautiful
Culture never encourages men to become harmful.

The Dog

Man's best companion the dog
It removes loneliness fog
Always better than the hog
You can write in the blog
Friendship will never clog
To make you happy dog will slog;
Dog will never betray master
Bark at enemy coming nearer
To protect you fight like soldier
Always follow you wherever
Wait for you even in hunger
Pet a dog as your partner.

Cunning

Cunning people are skilled in deceit
Self-interest is always their ambit
Clever in deceiving even best friend
For propaganda they are rightly trained;
Cunning people instigate others to fight
But always try to make self-interest bright
Don't allow cunning people to make you tight
Avoiding cunning friends is good and right.

Current

Flow of electricity is called current
If you touch it you will get death warrant;
Current also means present time
Keep your current assets always fine;
Current account is important in business
If you can't meet current liabilities face disgrace;
Life is nothing but combination of current moment
If you lose current time your lose your improvement.

Money Has Relative Value

Money has only relative value
Necessity determines it
When you are in a troubled pit
Even a small amount cam fit
Money has no absolute writ;
If you are in hospital bed every penny count
Even though your bill may be small amount
Without money you will be nowhere around
To pay hospital bills you are legally bound
The value of money gives you good sound;
When you give money you know it's importance
While receiving everybody show ignorance
After lending money receiver will forget
In coming days the lender will only regret
Money has different value in the same basket.

Cynic

Cynic says people are selfish
Self-interest no need to teach
Others right people breach
Own interest always preach;
Yet we see lot of selfless people
Their lifestyle is very simple
They serve society but humble
Help others during trouble;
Philanthropy is still surviving
Donations people are providing
For others pain lot of people are crying
Cynicism itself selfishness but nothing.

Alcohol

Alcohol is a good drink
As long as you don't sink
After three pegs always think
Otherwise you lose your link
Your colour will change to pink
Soon you will be on the brink
Looking you wife will start to wink
Life will reach a uncertain kink
Alcohol is always a helpful drink.

Tree And Me

I asked the tree, how is life treating you?

The tree replied, excellent, I am enjoying life happily

The sun is supplying rays as usual and wind carbon dioxide

The cloud is providing rainwater when needed

My chlorophyll is busy in photosynthesis to make food

The birds are busy constricting nest to lay eggs

The honeybees are busy coming and going to collect nectar

The queen bee is laying eggs very fast to pollinate wheat in coming season

The inserts on the branches are playing beautiful music for me

And you are living because, I am supplying you oxygen

Yet, you have no respect for me and invented motorized saw

Your forefathers, never harmed us, as you modern people are doing

One tree equal to hundred sons, they used to say

Your modern selfish generation knew nothing, except me, me and me

But always remember, your me is alive because of tree.

The Ladder Of Death

Every moment, we are climbing the ladder of death

Neither we can stop, nor we can go down to bottom

We can only move upward, fall down or jump to instant demise

Even if we reach the top, there is no different prize

Only the number of years will represent a longevity tag

No use of hundred years, as in the end, empty will be our bag

Enjoy every step of the ladder without fear of fall

When time comes, you can't go upward but to take the call

In the domain of time, our period of existence is small

Make your today cheerful and happy, not fire ball.

Say Goodbye!

People stuck up in the skin deep beauty

Soon they realize their mistake and reality

Between them, they can't find any compatibility

Even living together, life becomes solitary

The beauty of first sight vanishes without any reason

The journey of life together becomes a prison

Separation, quarrel and divorce remain as only solution

Sometimes killing of partner puts other one in prison

Running after skin deep beauty as love at first sight may be dangerous

Dating in restaurants, pubs and Cafe for some time is smarter

Slowly, you can see the inner beauty through your third eye

When you find ugliness inside, you can easily say goodbye.

Beauty Is Everywhere

Beauty is there on the small drops of rain

When it falls on the dust, a thing it paints

The falling of rain drops on grass is another beauty

During rain standing under a big tree see the rains vanity

As the rain stops, the beautiful rainbow comes

Quietly some butterfly appears from somewhere and dance

Looking to the sky, the white and black clouds starts to play

The naughty wind does not allow to be static and stay

The clouds move on and on making a different beauty

Only observation needed to make a poem salutary

Beauty lies everywhere, don't think a raindrop, ordinary

You can see beauty in everywhere and every creation

To see beauty from inner eyes should be your intention.

British, The Exploiter

British have not only exploited wealth from India

But also saved the Hindu culture from extinction

Railway line and telegraph was the credit of the company

The quarrelling small kingdoms learned to live in harmony

The forceful conversion to Islam came to a halt

Though removal of traditional education is cultural bolt;

Without British, India would have been an Islamic country

The British government changed the Mughal's game

The Hindu didn't try to regroup and fight the Delhi's king

Rather, busy in fighting among to retain own Thorn

Thank God, with arrival of British a new culture born

They never tried for forcible conversion to Christianity

Through education, with all religious groups they made solidarity

Business was their prime motive to rule India through division

To control a caste, creed, religion divided that was only solution

Before British, Northeast was not part of Mughal rule

To merge with India was British's administrative tool

For exploiting Indian wealth, they made lot of atrocities

But allowing survival of Hindu way is a big reciprocity

Today the Hinduism is flourishing for the liberal people

Without proper analysis, writing off contributions is harmful.

Love And Death

They got married after several years of love
Living without one another was impossible
Yet, the honeymoon was over too quickly
To grab his property, she played the drama
His new girlfriend tried to get rid of her
The rat race started under the mask with smile
The survival of the fittest is always the game
Motivating a frustrated unemployed was easy for a girl
With one night stand he became crazy her
The husband got his freedom at midnight
Disposing the dead body is a task tight
Easy to cut into pieces and throw in jungle
For ever, wild animals will dispose trouble
One small mistake made the story tragic for the new pair
In jail the same cell they are not allowed to share.

The Holes

For good health, clean mouth and teeth are necessary

But, taking care of one hole called mouth, don't forget others

Asshole is equally important for a good health

Piles, fistula, fissures and constipation can make life miserable

If your nose holes are closed, you are in real trouble

The cleaning of ear holes is important for listening

The small holes of eyes are necessary for crying

The holes of genital parts are not only for urination

These holes are vital for survival of human civilization

If you can keep your holes perfect and healthy

Good health will accompany you continuously.

Are We Witnessing Trailers?

He killed his girlfriend and made her body pieces

She killed her husband and did the same thing

How can live be so cruel and deadly, we can't imagine

Isn't it burial of love and relationships for money

Or there was never love, only lust and sexual desire

People find it difficult to kill their pet dog and cat

Very strange, how one can killed the one whom they love

The humanity at low ebb and values totally broke down

The civilized society can't move like this for long

The collapse may be nearing, and we are witnessing trailers.

An Outdated Soul

They met for the first time in the fast food cafe

Love at first sight, Facebook status changed to engaged

They celebrated with friends in the college canteen

Loiter in the nearby park and hug each other

After few weeks suddenly status of both changed to single

The photos of intimate moments disappeared

They seat in the cafe, as if they have never met each other

One week after he met his soul mate and she hers

Status again changed from single to engaged

Both of them celebrated separately with same group of friends

No one knows how long Facebook status and photos will remain

I always looked at them, and cry for my departed wife

With whom I used to be visit the cafe together

Am I an outdated soul or like Alice in wonderland?

I asked myself, yesterday, today, and maybe tomorrow again.

Man Proposes, God Disposes!

Man proposes God disposes

But his all disposals are not fair

We were taught by religion not question

If we go on asking questions, there will be no solution

The authority of God will get diluted

People will destroy Mosque, Church and temple

Society will no longer remain stable and humble

Even with fear of God, so much of violence

War between countries in each religion is abundance

So, the priests teaches that we should surrender

If we question God's wrong decisions, that is unfair

Civilization has flourished and gone to oblivion

But people are afraid to ask God, pertinent question

Who proposes for dogs, foxes and donkey is uncertain

For their lives, does God has no purpose and reason

As long as there is death, associated with birth

All powerful invisible God will always show might.

Life Is A Tragic Play

I think, life is a tragic play, once role is over we must leave

I think life is a rented house, we must vacate once the owner told

I think, life a journey, only the train guard knows where to get down

Sometimes I think, life is a earthen pot, any moment may break

Is life a water drop on lotus leaf, any moment can vanish

Whatever way we call life, it is totally uncertain

Today's sunshine is the only beautiful life's gain

Yesterday is already gone to the irreversible position

For tomorrow also we don't have any fixed resolution

One moments accident can change life till death

The bold and mighty also forced to lie on hospital bed

Whatever life maybe, just play your role sincerely

At death bed no point in crying unnecessarily.

Enjoy Silence For A Day Or Two

I took out my coloured glasses

So green the beautiful grasses

The horizon is beyond imagination

As I walked through the woods

I removed my wireless ear phones

The sounds of the insects was heavenly

The birds were singing without bothering,

About the lonely homosapian in their territory

They might be knowing, killing wild birds is now illegal

Or homosapian without any weapon is powerless

The sound of the tiny spring is clearly audible

No need of manmade amplifier or gadgets

There was no silence, yet absolute silence

The silence, which I was searching for a long in madding crowd

Throw away your gadget for a day, and enjoy silence.

Don't Pray For Gain

Neither I have seen him nor heard his voice

I have not touched him no felt his presence

Why should I pray him and for what purpose

Whether I pray him or don't pray him, things will happen

Neither earthquake nor flood will stop coming

Even if he has the power, he is powerless to save the dear one

No dead man will come out of grave even billions pray

My prayers are immaterial to the solar system

Also, my prayers are not at useful to mankind and society

It helps only the weak-minded human, who is afraid to die

Instead of prayers, let me cry alone to lighten pain

No need to pray to unknown if you pray for a gain.

Don't Wait, Make Your Bust Today

My yesterday was my present, yesterday
So, my past and present are good today
Every day comes as today and becomes past
Yesterday's future today will also not last
Last year's memory will also slowly gather dust
Only the sweet and beautiful memories will not rust
For a better tomorrow, foundations today cast
To build a better tomorrow, strong foundation must
Later on, your good words on future, no one will trust
With courage and confidence today is time to bast
If you are already forty plus, you should walk fast
Open your windows, and see, opportunities are vast
If you work today, future will certainly make your bust.

Strong Man Doesn't Cry

They said, strong man doesn't cry like children

But, man or woman, pain gives the same burden

The tears flow naturally when we are in grief

The wrong notion put unnecessary pressure in heart

People resist tears even is for sadness it naturally start;

If strong man is not allowed to cry, they will become angry

Out of frustration for some one's blood, they will be hungry

The strongest man always has the kindest heart

Let him allow to shed tears freely, when it starts

After crying freely and continuously, he will again be smart.

Love Is Not In The Hand Of God Now

Love depends on caste, career, beauty and bank balance

Love at first sight now a days has no perseverance

Living together is for mutual benefits and sharing expenses

When the matter of marriage comes, strong one gives resistance

The omnipotent God has lost his heavenly importance;

Gay and lesbian can live together without increasing expenses

So, generally, their living together has persistence

Marriage becoming costly due to costly upkeep of children

More than one child means, difficulties in quality education

For good health care, insurance coverage alone not solution.

Infidelity

Infinite sexual desire of human mind
Pushes human to another partner
The Infidelity creates havoc in family
People killed their partner even in suspicion
Many flourishing kingdoms pushed to ruin
Yet, infidelity was, is and will be there in society
Mentally, man is not a monogamous animal
Though, customs and society forced to be social
Keeping concubine was the practice of the rich
Infidelity now loses sharpness, new concept society to teach.

Shiva The Destroyer

Shiva, the other side of the coin called life

Even being the ultimate truth, every one is afraid of

But accidentally many people meet the truth soon

That may the reason why Shiva is known for unpredictable action

The ultimate truth is always a process irreversible;

One day even the world will come to the end

Anti matter from his third eye will bloom

In solar system, there will be no earth, sun or moon

In the new systems, there may not be midnights and noon

The law of existence and destruction may not be common.

Health Alone Is Not Wealth

Physical health is wealth is true

But for a mad man it is untrue

Mental health is more important

Wealth of Stephen Hawkins pertinent

Without mental health life is impotent;

Dynamic equilibrium of body and mind is real health

Unbalance of body and mind will make life filth

Majority of people are not bothered to strengthen mind

So, even with health, happiness and joy they can't find

For a better life, potential of your mind try to unwind.

Climbing Everest Is Easy

Climbing Everest is easy
If for it, your mind is crazy
Practicing it, you should be busy
To reach peak, never be lazy
Otherwise, Everest will be hazy;
To achieve goal attitude is important
Practice leads you towards perfection
Without hard work, for result no solution
For hard work you need determination
Attitude, hard work will take you to destination.

Widows Of Vrindavana (Brindaban)

They are living, because basic instinct of life is to live

Far away from the family and friends once they used to love

No one is in the world to share their emotions or wife tears

No one is there to empower them to lead towards a better life

Yet, they living without hope to complete the journey;

The religious leaders are silent about their plight

For them their is no human rights, only prayer is the path

Except death what they can ask from the all powerful God

Along with the death of their husband has also abandoned

Their only life is the past, no present, how they will have a tomorrow?

Christ

The title given to son of God Jesus
He was messiah of mediaeval mass
People listen to his teaching and trust
'Hate sin not sinner' his words robust
Propagated peace and love among people
But the job among hostile people not simple
Crucified by the people who didn't believe
With reincarnation he gave world relief
The Testament is his recorded speaking
Christianity has changed people's thinking
Christ sacrificed his life for mankind
Live and let live his teaching always remind.

He Sacrificed Life

Only Jesus sacrificed own life
He didn't merry several wife
Because of him peace is prevailing
The mankind got path of smooth sailing
Otherwise violence would have boiling;
Jesus showed the path of love
So we saw flying peace of dove
He prayed for those who crucified him
Hate the sin not sinner his teaching theme
Without Jesus world will be lame.

Cross

Jesus was crucified on holy cross
Injustice to son of God was gross
Jesus's certification mankind's loss;
Cross is the mixture of two things
Better products cross breed brings
Cross fire may hit your own bird's wings;
Cross section is important in engineering
Marathon is long cross country running
Dating of object by co relation is cross- dating;
Multiplication is also known as cross product
Many a times sure goal cross bar obstruct
Earn your cross through hard work and good conduct.

Christmas

The annual Christian festival
The date of Jesus Christ arrival
Santa Claus gave the good news
The world covered with white dews
Ding-dong bell sounds Jesus is coming
Festivity mood with Carol starts booming
The star and cross glow in every church
Christmas a milestone in humanity march.

Church

The building of universal prayer
All humans are welcome there
Such a place of humanity rare
The holy cross reminds supreme sacrifice
Love the mankind it always describe
Church symbolises human values
Peace and brotherhood it deluge
The atmosphere gives tranquillity to mind
Anxiety, tension, sadness one can unwind
The morning bell ring remind a good day
The teaching of Jesus proudly it say.

He Made This

He made this world full of pain
Our prayers mostly go in vain
Tears come from eyes like drain
His mission is to clean heart main
He pulled up when we fall in drain
Everything he binds with fine chain
Without pain no one can gain
He has given every man a brain
His son came to the world to train.

My God Died Young

My God died young
His teaching always strong
We love Christmas Carol song
Journey to sainthood is long;
Love and peace road to salvation
In every walk of life there is satisfaction
The path of Jesus need determination
But to follow him don't have hesitation;
God sent his son to make world beautiful
Jesus stop Satan making man sinful
So Jesus was crucified with cruelty
Yet he prayed for forgiveness boldly;
Jesus's teaching is still showing light
One day world will become heavenly bright
Man will give up hate, violence and fight
Follow Jesus's path mankind will be right.

Buddhism

The religion that teaches nonviolence
The war hungry world it can only silence
Ashok the great embrace one day Buddhism
He gave up life's all types of cynicism
Propagated peace and brotherhood in world
Buddha's greatness to the world he unfold
The eight-fold path can show human light
Following Buddha's teaching make world bright.

Messenger Of Peace

Buddha, the messenger of peace
To the world nonviolence he teach
All nook and corner his message reach
Millions of people now Buddhism preach;
Buddha gave noble eightfold path to practice
To the mankind his teaching can give justice
Buddhism follows the middle path without friction
The noble eightfold path leads to liberation
Right view, right intention, right speech, right action
Right livelihood, effort, mindfulness, samadhi give salvation
In today's world Buddhism became more pertinent
Let us make Buddha's noble eightfold path more prominent.

Dalai Lama

Spiritual head of Tibetan Buddhism
Main opponent of Chinese communism
Now mascot for world pluralism
Always advocate social secularism;
Independent Tibet was once his dream
His mission China already trim
Hope of independent Tibet very slim
Propagating peace his beautiful cream;
Nobel peace prize already he own
Nonviolence path he has shown
People gave him lovely crown
His visit is always talk of the town.

Traveling

If you want to travel fast and far
Traveling light is better and comfortable
Only your GPS and maps should be reliable
Heavy luggage is always a burden in travel
Sleeping bag and rucksack are better companion
To know a place, cycling and walking better solution;
If you have not seen the great wall, you have seen nothing
Taj Mahal is really wonderful to see something
Eiffel tower may not be your point of interest
But a journey through the Canadian Rockies is best
In Sonmarg, Gulmarg, and Mount Titlis take little rest.

Daddy

Paying children's bills
Daddy becomes dad
For children he is mad;
Scold by wife every day
To children no, never say
Child is his smiling ray;
Sacrifice many hobbies
End life in family lobbies
In children see new promise;
Banker for children, porter for wife
Always busy to make children's life
For daddy children should strive.

Dance

One of the oldest forms of art
Dance is always cultures part
In early life dancing lesson start
Dancing couples are every smart;
Dance little baby dance with music
Steps in sequence is the basic
Move in a quick lively synchronize way
To enjoy the dance show people will pay;
Dance band is playing in the dance hall
Come to the dancing floor O' baby dall
Don't wait smiling for partners call
Maintain your steps and rhythm not to fall.

Danger

The possibility of suffering injury
More dangerous is friends perjury
Danger is possibility of causing harm
To face danger be prepared and firm;
Every walk of life is full of unknown danger
So practice to become a skilled ranger
Brave people overcome fighting face to face
Don't run fearing danger away from life's race;
Danger is always associated with adventure
While climbing Everest you may lost life there
While travelling through jungle take utmost care
Any moment dangerous lion may come and roar.

Past

Don't regret for the past
It has already gathered rust
Present will also not last
Utilization of it must
Start working for future fast;
Soon present will gather dust
Future has no definite trust
Anything unpleasant it may cast
Next hour your bubble may burst
Make present beautiful and just;
Forget about your past mistake
Your present past should not dictate
Only carry the experience you gather
Keep your sweet memory as feather
Work and enjoy the present without bother.

Caste System

A peculiar social disorder in India
Upper caste suffer superiority phobia
Once lower caste were untouchable
But now they are a force formidable
But caste system is still insoluble;
Brahmins propagated caste system
With it now job reservation is in tandem
In marriage caste is prime consideration
This leads to higher caste glorification
Inter caste marriage still insubordination;
Caste system is now a political tool
Through politics of caste government rule
Caste struggle became vested interest
For caste less society many people protest
On cross road Indian democracy rest.

Benchmark

To achieve higher level benchmark is necessary
For success in business and sports it is mandatory
Without benchmark you cannot think higher
With benchmark your mind and spirit get fire
In every walk of life benchmark always inspire
Without benchmark success in modern business rare
Benchmark is not merely a management tool
To achieve higher level of success make it rule.

Bipolar World

Nature made world bipolar, South and North
Man-made polarity not a matter of worth
Once world became bipolar Hitler and rest
In Osama versus rest bipolarity now rest
Though Osama is dead thousands alive
In Pakistan, Afghanistan, Iraq they strive
Bipolarity is good for nature not for society
Osama's followers should accept diversity.

Black And White

In the colourful world
Black and white still rule
Without black and white
People may make us fool
Signature is protection tool
Black and white is antique
Better than colourful boutique
The night is black, day is white
Black and white makes others bright.

Black Hole

Gravitational force is at extreme
Star became invisible supreme
Nothing can escape black hole
Absorbing everything its only role
The event horizon starts there
Even seeing light can be rare
Be like black hole to absorb criticism
You can overcome others cynicism.

Do A Memorable Job Today

Today do a memorable job for other
S/he will remember you like father
Be a friend to a person who is in need
Next year, this day, you will feel great in deed
If you can't do nothing, a street dog you can feed;
Today with become past tomorrow morning
First day of every month we should think as warning
Today only you can take the required turning
Tomorrow you may face an issue that is burning
Today's action can only make tomorrow shining.

Climate Change Is Disturbing

Whether anyone believes in God or not is immaterial

The debate for and against God is from time immemorial

Both the sides have in their favour mountain like material

Even for Gautam Buddha, the problem was perennial

Let the dispute be between the God and the individual;

Buddha himself flip flopped about God's existence

But all other prophets in favour of God showed persistence

Whether there is God or no God, entropy of universe is increasing

Through war and violence, the mankind is disintegrating

For mankind, the advent of climate change is disturbing.

So Insignificant We Are

Now I realize how insignificant me and she
But still in darkness, where is our life's key
Society didn't not bother whether we are dead
Too soon, our existence from people fade
But to contribute for society, we were mad;
If people realize the truth soon is good
At death bed, nothing will destroy mood
It does not mean to people we should be rude
Without any expectation, to poor, serve food
People still remember Jesus and the rood.

Reasons Many

For selfish reasons we behave irrational
Hunger and greed make us criminal
For safety and security, we become social
To remain in the power, we are political
Sometimes, our activities are whimsical;
Animal instincts in human life is many
We behave sometimes like donkey
Sometimes our attitude is like monkey
Sometimes we become a tiger, lonely
To change our behaviour, reasons many.

Mistake

Mistake after mistake, mistake after mistake
All mistakes, our free will always dictate
Doing wrong is part of our life's journey
Penalty kick is also part of the tourney
Don't count profit and loss in terms of money;
We learn more from mistake than success
But lessons must be learnt in the process
If we do not learn, there will be no progress
Same mistake, again we will fail to address
Journey of life will be burden and endless.

Our Existence

Our existence is in matter, energy, space and time
Gravity and electromagnetic forces are prime
Strong and weak nuclear forces are the seed of time
The yardstick of measuring all is our own creation
A fundamental theory of everything is still illusion;
God's sovereignty is beyond the four dimension
To prove the existence of God, so there is no solution
All theories about God are only human speculation
Human brain has some inherent difficulty and limitation
One day science will find out God through new civilization.

God And Nothing Of Physics

Something is better than nothing
From nothing, how can come everything
If nothing can create galaxy like something
Why is something required to born living being?
Even in marriage, we exchange finger ring;
Some people claimed, they were sent by God as king
To glorify prophets, millions of people always sign
In between something and nothing, life always swing
When we try to know the truth, it always sting
Common people have no alternative other than praying.

Inquisitiveness

Inquisitiveness is generally genetical
Sometimes it happens to be circumstantial
It is also induced by factors, environmental
For some, it is to gain milage political
But Inquisitiveness is never unethical;
Innovation is induced by inquisitiveness
Innovative people never feel loneliness
In every step, new ideas, they witness
They are human beings with openness
To question in every matter, their weaknesses.

Not Everything Matters Of Science

Ethics is not a matter of science and technology
It is only perception of life and philosophy
Science has no formula for ethical conduct
Ethics is considered to be sociological product
Emotions and feelings can't be laboratory by-product;
Every aspect of life is not in the domain of science
Scientific hypothesis cannot determine romance
Without explanation, love and lovemaking advance
Science can only provide air-conditioned ambience
I love you is not à formula, but emotional sentence.

Purpose Of Life

The purpose of life is too difficult to describe

Better mission, goals and objectives to subscribe

We never know why we came and why we go

Life is temporary like a water bubble that glow

Sometimes it flies high and sometimes very low;

Striving for a better-quality life may be goal and objective

Mission of doing good to mankind and nature is positive

The purpose of life always a matter remains as subjective

The purpose of life as per religion and science is not cognitive

So, for majority of people earning money for comfort is lucrative.

Purpose Of Life-2

For human, there is no purpose of life
If you don't have husband or wife
Though marriage is double edge knife
Without any fruit, single life wipe
So, unmarried life is only a life's prototype;
Married life has too many purpose
Whole life you have to work to dispose
Every day, new purpose situation will impose
Sometimes for divorce you may propose
But living alone will not give diversity, I suppose.

Blame Game

Success has many fathers' failure is orphan

In failure everyone plays blame game organ

In every failure blame game is best defence

Throw away blame game if you want success

After the match is over blame game divide people

Post-mortem should be objective and simple

In corporate blame game is skin saving tool

But with blame game every time you can't make others fool.

Blessing

Blessings many times come in disguise
Before we see or realise it subside
In every problem we pray for blessing
But without work blessing give nothing
Yet blessing is positive fore can do good
That is why blessing is always mental food
When we ask God's blessing, we get strength
Blessing others in trouble times always worth.

Blotting Paper

Down the memory lane
Still remember the thick paper
Carried to school with fountain pen
Absorb excess ink while writing
To keep our notebook shining
Technology itself stopped excess ink
Blotting paper lost its student link.

Bluetooth

Bluetooth once united Denmark Norway
But he is now in history far away
Modern Bluetooth made him sway
Today's Bluetooth is like runaway
Interconnect mobile phone without wire
Made communication technology fair
In computer networks it has good share
Without Bluetooth gen-X handicapped
The ghost of Bluetooth so shaped.

Boat

One of the earliest transports is boat
Because on water it can easily float
Boat doesn't need any road to travel
The current of water even can propel
Like nomad's boat people also spread
In spreading civilization boat is a thread
Without boat British Empire was nothing
Through boat only once it was spreading
Boat is not only for Crossing River and lake
Transportation of goods it always make
The modern version of boat ship is big
Yet still boat can give ship a dig
The Fisherman boat will always stay
We are on the same boat brothers let us say.

Anger

When anger boil
Throw it on soil
Life it will spoil
Stop the heating coil
Anger spill venom
Reverse count random
Anger control must
Before it burst
Make it small dust
Spill water to rust
It will lose on crust.

If You Are Right

If you are right
Don't take it light
Make it bright
Show your might
If required fight
Forcefully bite
Fly like kite
Don't afraid night
You will see light
Because you are right.

Body Language

When you can't speak
Your mind is meek
Heart can't take risk
Body language click
Communication may not be loud
It may not make any sound
Writing is not bound
Solution body language can found
Union of two happens through eye
To communicate the children cry
With gloomy face wife remain shy
Body language can make life dry
Raise your hand when required
Otherwise, you will not move forward
Body language can bring you reward
In interviews show the right gesture
Walking confidently important signature
Bold leader's body language is armature
Learning body language important
Speaking, writing alone can't make you competent.

You Are Bold

I know you are strong and bold
You are precious than gold
You can't be bought and sold
Even with heat you can't be rolled
Your courage everyone told
Even in windy days not cold
Only with love you can be mould
With respect and smile you can be fold
Because I know you are strong and bold.

Bonus

Smile comes when heard about bonus
For pocket it is opposite to minus
Bonus is not hard earned or lottery
Yet to encourage work it is flattery
Without bonus festivals are dull and dry
For corporate management it is hot fry
In share market bonus issues are welcome
To appease shareholders, it is a premium
In every walk of life, we expect little bonus
The person introducing it motivating genius.

Booby Trap

Why it is called booby trap
The explosion is worse than rape
Boobs are soft and beautiful
Trap is dangerous and harmful
Touching booby trap will kill
But beautiful boobs always thrill
Some king might have lost war
Looking for beauty in country far
Rakhi Sawant had donated her two
That is why explosive trap called so.

Brainstorm

Idle brain devil's workshop
In brainstorming it works
Brainstorm is to find solution
Problem has path for dilution
Brainstorming is great discussion
Everyone has opportunity for submission
Sometimes it cracks hard nut
Though there may be ifs and but
Even though no result in brainstorming session
Tea coffee and good snacks participation commission.

Bribe

For human greed and lust bribe strive
Without genetic engineering it will alive
Bribe is now part of our day-to-day life
For government job done it is Swiss knife
In office no bribe no work is the rule of law
In front of officer's gift courtesy, one must show
On bribe the media made lot of hue and cry
While taking money for paid news they aren't shy
In taking bribe politicians are not alone
The whole society is their good companion
Bribe now flows in our blood to carry oxygen
Without bribe Indian society will go to hibernation.

Brain Drain

Brain drain is phenomenon natural
From village to city people travel
Skilled people look for better opportunity
Brainy people seek another possibility
Brain drain helped progress of mankind
Many brain would have remained unwind
Brain drain creates non-resident citizen
To the mother land it brings new kaizen
For countries brain drain brings foreign exchange
Economy of poor country brain drain can change
Brain drain mixes the people with best culture
United humanity they create can never rupture .

Bridge

On big river and ocean, we make bridge
To connect people, it is utmost need
Without bridges roads are lame duck
Through bridges cross food carrying truck
Concrete bridges we made so much
Every road is now full of year around rush
It is now time to bridge men's metal gap
So that we can have one world road map
Let us make bridges between religion
The people of world will see new horizon
Let us make bridges between culture
There will be no hatred and war in future
Internet is now the infinite bridge of unity
Use it to carry love and peace for humanity.

Brief

We came to world for a brief period
You have to go even if you use steroid
Be brief in every walk of life and work
You will get enough time to enjoy pork
If you don't become brief you will carry load
You will suffer misery and pain on bumpy road
Briefcase is better compared to a trunk
In journeys no need to carry every junk
While leaving we can't even carry brief case
So why so much greed in life's brief race.

Bull

Take the bull by the horn
Otherwise, you have to mourn
Always ignore bullshit in life
Bullish days will then strive
For your right make bullfight
In this world bullet is right
Bulldog can be good companion
Bullion can make you champion
Bull shot may be a good drink
Don't bully weak and the pink.

Buoyant

In life always be buoyant
Never say any time I cannot
Cheerful and optimistic can win
To face challenges, they are keen
Buoyancy keeps you always afloat
Safely you can sail your life's boat
Buoyant people has determination
God never do with them discrimination.

No One Is Indispensable

No one is indispensable in the world
Successor time will automatically unfold
When Indira Gandhi was gunned down
Successor of Prime Minister was easily found
Pilot could navigate India so sound
Rabri Devi came out of kitchen and ruled Bihar
Rubber stamp Prime Minister Mano Mohan was there
We forgot who Governor before Urjit Patel was
TN Sheshan is not known by many though he faught battle
Governor will come and Governor will go
Only requirement is that economy should flow and grow.

Atom

Smallest part of an element is atom
Made of neutron electron and proton
Though tiny it has immense energy
Atom's combination is matters synergy
Bohr has developed an atom model
Atom is invisible unlike lightning candle
Hydrogen and oxygen atoms give water
Without water no living beings will be there.

Café

Not merely a coffee house
Many ideas cafe rouse
New startup it arouse
Loneliness cafe douse
Not merely a place to fill belly
It is an enjoyable place really
Youngsters make rally
Budget also always tally
Single one's destination finally
Meet your friends there certainly.

Cadet

O' thy young cadet
Focus on your target
Your mission don't forget
Make your life largest
March-past, March-past
Always move very fast
You have to travel vast
Don't be lazy and last
Make bigger your bust
Don't gather any rust
March-past, March-past.

Butterfly

With colourful small wings
Red, yellow, white, blue and green
Flying from flower to flower seen
Always busy and like restless teen
Sitting on bushes make a rainbow
Their flying range is very narrow
Not worried what will happen tomorrow
Even if don't get nectar do not feel sorrow
Make season colourful with their presence
During snowy winter feel butterflies absence.

Butterfly Chasing

Promotion is like colourful butterfly
When we chase, it flies in to the sky
We became depressed and sit shy
To catch it after a while again we try
Flying here and there it say bye bye
Then we take rest becoming tired
Think in mind butterfly is not required
Suddenly butterfly rests on our shoulder
In another location we open new folder
Life and promotion is butterfly chasing
When you seat coolly it return for igniting.

Cake

Don't want to eat the cake and have it too
It will bend your backbone like a bow
Eat and enjoy the cake when you have time
On the baking day cakes are always fine
Tomorrow you may not be alive to dine
Birthday without cake is incomplete
Cut the cake and eat it with friends complete
If you hold cake for too long, it will gather moss
The taste of the icing cake forever will loss
Enjoy your bonus and incentive travelling abroad
Otherwise, someone will take out through ATM fraud.

Calendar

Days, weeks, months and then year
To remind time calendar is here
The red dates remind take a holiday and rest
During the week you have performed your best
Calendar tells in the end one year has gone
Ask yourself how much job you have done
New calendar always give joy New Year has come
Proposals made this year I will do good job some
But time run fast in day-to-day affair
To the calendar we are always unfair.

Call Centre

Inside the call centre
The rule is hire and fire
No career you can desire
But lot of young they hire
Young blood is their attire
Computer and microphone
In the centre you are not alone
Any time service their backbone
That is why we can easily roam
To keep us smiling call centre foam
For a midnight call don't rudely scold
To call you someone might have told
So, you are in the call centre's fold
In digital world call centre is necessity
Inside a call centre you can see diversity
Different beautiful people are busy bee
One night at call centre peep and see.

Camel

The long necked tall animal with hump
In the deserts it can easily run and jump
Camel is known as the ship of desert
In Bedouin life came is indivisible part
Camel can live few days without water
For people in Arabia, it gives bread butter
Calm and quiet camel a domestic animal
Camel race in Arab countries a ritual
Don't use young boys in camel race
Discard it looking at their innocent face.

Camera

Ready smile and then a click
Cameras own identity bleak
For photographer it may stick
But common man doesn't pick
Before mobile camera is meek
Black and white camera is history
Kodak is caught inside boundary
For cinemas camera is still foundry
Youngsters are now selfie hungry
Camera will never get back old glory.

Cancer

Uncontrolled division of cell
Cancer makes one's life hell
Doctors say it is not a disease
Only division of cell it increase
Chemotherapy treatment painful
Radiation in long run harmful
Surgery always not successful
No curative medicine available
Prevention is not yet successful
Cancer management is costly
So, it is considered as ghostly
If detected early life can be saved
But reason of cancer to be solved.

Candle

The white cylindrical mass with a thread
The job and duty of it for mankind is great
Spreads light in the world since invention
Selfless service is candle's satisfaction
Before electricity came candle was king
Even now candle is a bright golden ring
Festival of light incomplete without candle
Candle is sold in the market as a bundle
In the graveyard we lit a candle for soul
Procession with candlelight always bold
Candle was once every shopkeeper sold.

Candy

The sweet sugar candy
For children it is brandy
Candies always trendy
To carry it is very handy
Enjoy candy when you're young
No candy after becoming strong
Diabetes hates candy most
Candy cannot make roast
Lollipop is popular for kid
For retired it has no need.

Canvas

The strong coarse unbleached cloth
Used to make sail and painting both
The beauty of canvas is in painting
Other activities of canvas lost shining
'The persistence of memory' reminds
In the 'Starry Night' 'Mona Lisa' shines
For millions of people canvas is lifeline
Selling canvases many painter dine
Without canvas no one can win election
In canvas auction market lot of selection
Put canvas painting on drawing room wall
The beauty of the house will be always tall.

Cap

The small cap on the head

Says always something

A message it bring

It is not merely for protecting

Sun ray dust or mountain dew

Festivity a cap renew

When we open the champagne cap

We enjoy the drink with music rap

For the young child cap is not only toy

Wearing it they run in joy

The upper limit is always a cap

Military cap can change a nation's map.

Capability

Elephant does not know own capability
So, elephant can be tamed
The tiger knows its capacity
So, the tiger is not servant lame
Know your own capability
Explore inherent capacity
You will accelerate velocity
For success knowing capability important
Enhancing capacity will give determination
Failed people don't know their inner power
Capacity building can bring them success shower.

Capital

Capital is the most important city
To govern the country capital's duty
Capitals are built with unique beauty
Presidential palace is symbol of unity
Invaders destroy capital as sign of victory
Protection of capital is so necessary
To start a business capital is important
For industrialisation capitalist pertinent
Capital punishment is the ultimate one
The economy now a days capitalist run.

Captain

You lead the team front
In high sea when tide hit the ship
You steer safely without fear
In the war front while facing enemy
You are never behind to save own life
O captain thy captain I salute you
A true captain never thinks for self
But lead the team to victory
When captain is bold, strong, and courageous
In the battlefield the troop is dangerous.

Caption

Captions are always important
What is inside remain subordinate
The first impression is last impression
If caption is good no need of tension
Caption can touch millions of heart
Everyone can carry caption in his cart
In marking caption can give good result
In politics caption is weapon of assault
Give a good caption to eventful life
In the journey it will be your cutting knife.

Carbon

The element of atomic number six
Existence of human civilization it will fix
With Hydrogen and Oxygen easily mix
Emission of too much carbon is a risk
Graphite and diamond its purest form
More carbon emission makes earth worm
Without carbon living thing is impossible
But too much of carbon made us vulnerable
Low carbon environment is need of the hour
In the carbon footprint new world will shower.

Environment

The progress of civilization is regress for environment
To save environment should be civilisation's commitment;
Nature's blunder is the creation of human in evolution
The mother earth is now incapable to find a solution
The man made civilization is the major cause of pollution;
Our ancestors till monkey has not destroyed ecology
After arrival of human started the destruction chronology
Human has to change its destructive psychology
Otherwise environment will destroy human biology.

Let The Tears Flow

Every drop of tear is also rain
Tear releases mental pain
Rain drops never go in vain
Mother earth always gain
Green grass grows in chain
Excess water flow through drain
Through evaporation again come rain;
The tears will wash all the dirt
New endeavour you can start
Evaporation will bring tears of joy
You can play with success toy
No need to stop tears under the mask
Allow it to flow, no need to keep under husk
After tears flow concentrate on your task.

Centre Of Life

Soil, water and air
To all always be fair
Biodiversity is rare
To preserve take care
Resources please share;
Sun is the centre life
Photosynthesis make it strive
Trees are the nucleus
Without tree rise Celsius
World will be full of virus;
Soil, water, air and sunlight
Together all environment right
Against imbalance we have to fight
Trees can only make environment bright
Sun will always give us free light.

Contraceptive

Contraceptive made women progressive
No need to remain submissive
Freedom from unwanted pregnancy
Helped country to improve literacy
World population contraceptive controlled
Progress of feminism it unfold
Contribution of contraceptive remain untold
It has contributed lot to make femininity bold.

Condom

Condom prevents pregnancy random
Against AIDS best prevention is condom
Between love and sex pregnancies fiefdom
For man using condom is the wisdom
In illiterate society condom is used seldom
So sex and population go in tandem;
God created man and woman, ordered them to multiply
Never thought that human will be in over supply
For reducing population explosion god ask for a reply
To save the world, condom so God deploy
For wide circulation condom patent no body apply
Condom now helps man to defy God's order to multiply.

Control

Control your anger
You will become stronger
Control your greed
Limited will be your need
Control your ego
Negativity will forgo
Control your tension
Easy will be situation
Control your jealousy
Better will become your policy
Control your emotion
You will see solution
Before you control other
Control self, dear brother.

Convert

Every moment we are converting
What I am just now is becoming
Time convert every moment to past
Nothing in the world remain ever last
Convert the raw materials to product
Your growth it will boldly induct
Convert your failure to pillar of success
In life every field of work you can progress
Sun convert hydrogen into helium
For nuclear power we convert uranium
Conversion always should be for better
For society and mankind it will matter.

Convenience

Freedom from effort and difficulty
Convenience give comfort sufficiently
Convenience improves efficiency
Inconvenience creates deficiency
Convenience stores every day destination
Getting everything nearby is satisfaction
Public convenience always keeps clean
If you make it dirty you are doing sin.

Conviction

When you have conviction

No place for contradiction
You can perform with dedication
Move forward with determination
Use all permutation and combination
Every problem will have solution
No need to indulge in insubordination
Never allow mind to go for hibernation
When you work for goal with conviction
Success will surely give satisfaction.

Cooperate

When we cooperate
We never regret
To help others is pleasure
It has no monetary measure
But for each other we care;
Cooperation develop team spirit
Teamwork is the success writ
Bull's eye together we can hit
Team will hold you from falling in pit
Make cooperation you winning kit.

Cook

Cook are the manufacturer of food
Without food no one have healthy look
Only after food you can read a book
Empty stomach can make you crook;
The beautiful smell of the kitchen
Makes one mouth-watering vixen
Hunger becomes self-driven
If the taste is bad heart is broken;
Every Cook is a Chemical engineer
Cooking is a chemical process forever
Catalyst salt, spices are always there
Pressure, temperature make cooking fair;
Cook can only make food delicious
Bad cook make dishes hilarious
Proportion of ingredients must be judicious
For restaurants Master Chef is precious.

Coordination

Bring the different elements into cohesion
For efficiency requirement is coordination
Work for better social, industrial relation
For coordination requirement is negotiation
Good coordinator always has intuition;
Coordination is necessary in every field
Without coordination better fruit never yield
To win a match coordination needed in field
International relations poor coordination shield
With better coordination disputes can be killed.

Copper

The red-brown metal carry electricity
In industry copper is necessity
Alloyed to form bronze and brass
Copper coins were once used by mass
In copper age copper ruled civilization
Later came bronze as a combination
Without copper no electricity, no electronics
Copper is an integral part of thermodynamics
Copper plates are still preserved as showpiece
Many people still use copper alloys in utensil and dish.

Companion

In the journey I am not alone
Everyone is of the same clone
Struggle to move forward
Failure and pain push backward
Yet everybody marching for reward
Disease, accident all is companion
The movement continues to become champion
In the long run reached the same destination
Why in the journey quarrel with companion?

Copycat

Copycat has now rule the world
Majority of people in copy paste fold
Duplicate of everything are now sold
Copycat also pretend they are bold
Even copy right their own they told;
Computer helped copycat boom
Originality has now faced doom
For silent innovator little room
Copycat can easily groom
Internet is copy cat's automatic loom;
China leads the copy paste movement
For copying they provide good solvent
Sufferer is the innovator innocent
Intellectual property right not potent
For success copy paste is good component.

Morning Shows The Day

Morning shows the day
Excellent will be today
Without hesitation I can say
So beautiful the morning ray
For the day none need to pay;
Every day is good and beautiful
Together we can make it fruitful
Violence can make the day harmful
When the day goes it will be painful
Let's make every day delightful.

Failure

Life may be full of failure
Consider them as trailer
Continue journey as sailor
Never become your own jailer;
Life is full of golden opportunity
To achieve goals, you need continuity
Don't stop your forward journey
Make your life a winning tourney;
Failure and success two sides of coin
Two sides perseverance can only join
When you make the upside down
You will find the winning crown.

Critics Will Never Appreciate

Critics will never appreciate

Leg puller will always depreciate

Beneficiaries will not authenticate

This does not mean; you will stop doing good

This does not mean to the critics you will be rude

This does not mean, to the hungry soul you will stop food

Move forward doing good till your last journey

Jesus was also crucified for spreading love in life's tourney

The path to search truth, love and God is painful

Move like Jesus the joy and peace of mind will be bountiful.

Correspondent

Correspondent report on regular basis
Many a time misleading their thesis
Half-truth they report for vested interest
Manipulation causes to many disgust
Drawing room correspondents are broker
Once upon a time they were news hacker
Good correspondents are straight, fearless
In public interest no one should be careless
True correspondent report facts and truth
War and crime reporting difficult even for youth
Justice can be given by correspondent through honesty
To uphold truth should be correspondent's polity.

Corrupt

Evil and morally depraved are corrupt
Dishonestly money they accept
But their downfall comes abrupt
Corrupt people are always greedy
They never bother for the needy
In third world corruption is rule of law
Society is under corrupt people's jaw
Corruption is destroying religion and culture
Corrupt people are eating nation's wealth like vulture.

Jungle

The nature in its perfect balance
The struggle is to defeat nature's challenge
Survival of the fittest is the law
Even the weakest animal we saw
The lion never kills unnecessarily
Deer survives in jungle successfully
The biodiversity maintain survival of all
Many trees become so very tall
Supreme animal is the cause of fall
Destruction of jungle let us stall.

My Inconsistent Mind

O my inconsistent mind
Right path easy to find
Why move like a blind
The right path is, to be kind
Greed, jealousy to be wind;
When we shed tears for others
We feel like their brothers
Joy of helping is matter to feel
The inconsistency it can kill
Mind can think to move with zeal;
Service to man is service to God
Its satisfaction is better than iPod
Mind becomes strong like iron rod
Look to down and help the needy
Mind will never allow to be greedy.

Proud

Don't be proud of wealth
Don't be proud of health
Any moment may stop breath
Any moment may come death
So why choose imposing path;
Health and wealth all are temporary
They will not remain your contemporary
Health is wealth, money is supplementary
Life is bounded by a limited boundary
Proud is a negative force and reactionary.

We Are Actor

Death will come, it is certain
It will lower the stage curtain
For the best role you must bargain
Your performance you have to maintain
Unwanted dialogue one must restrain;
In the stage of world, we all are actor
Individually we are not at all a factor
Even though you are a powerful rector
Plough the soil with your tractor
For a weak soul become a mentor;
However insignificant your role may be
God wishes your best performance to see
You may have to give oxygen like a tree
Yet be thank to the Lord and bend your knee
Our duty is to play our role like honey bee.

Religion

Religion is opium
Yet it's like uranium
When enriched premium
Otherwise raw sodium
Cause fire to stop momentum
Religion needs coating of chromium;
Religion is mass hysteria
Though love and peace is its criteria
Spoiling the society like bacteria
Never become like Cross Victoria
Caused in world only diarrhoea.

Religion And Politics

Religion and politics are two sides of the coin
Behind the scene hands both of them join
Both are powerful tool to exploit poor
Protesters can be easily shown the door
In power game one complements other
Religion and politics are true twin brother
Both swear in the name of their father God
But their basic intention is to do fraud
In the power game common people are pony
Politicians and priest always drink honey.

Zoom

Zoom your horizon
Don't be confined in zoo
Close the zip of friction
Wider vision will give satisfaction;
Zone, zodiac all imaginary
Delete all those are reactionary
Make your zooming satisfactory
Everything you see are momentary;
Zoom and zoom to the sky
The universe will make you fly
Petty things will disappear
Through zooming life will be happier.

I Want To Be A Kid

I am never satisfied with need
I want to fulfil my infinite greed
Every moment I saw new seed
So, life is full of variety of breed
To nurture all a difficult deed
Yet the greedy mind never heed
A new wish mind everyday feed
O God, help me to remove weed
Let me go back and become a kid.

Father's Day

Every morning he looks to her face
Then he goes out for the race
He has to work every day with same pace
For his daughter he has to build a base;
When he comes back, she remains asleep
To her beautiful face with smile he peep
His love for her in the heart is very deep
The promises he made he must keep;
The burden to keep her smiling may be heavy
But he considered it to be his privy
He was never an expressive savvy
But carrying load his backbone became curvy;
No one listens to his inner pain
He sacrifices everything for her gain
Bind his emotions with iron chain
On her success his tears fall like rain.

Yacht

Light sailing racing boat
For wind power it wears coat
Only rich can afford the luxury
Before buying yacht fill your treasury
For sailing in rough sea skill is required
Without skill in hostile sea don't go forward
The yacht journey is always wonderful
Your yachtsman should be playful
On harbour yachts looks beautiful
In the cockpit one must be skilful.

Yoga

Not only good for body and soul
It can improve living as a whole
Yoga is not merely an exercise
It gives resistance against disease
When you inhale more oxygen in
The chances of heart problem thin
Yoga gives flexibility to muscle
Your whole body becomes flexible
When you make yoga your companion
With good health you become champion.

Today Is Best Day To Feel Happy

Cherry blossom only to fall down
Next year again we can found
Year after year it makes round
To come again cherry is duty bound
Never cherry blossom make any sound;
The beautiful flower bloom for few days
Flower knows soon it will lose colourful rays
Enjoy the beauty and fragrance today it says
Any moment wind may blow away the petal
As a dry useless piece the flower may settle;
Life is also same, enjoy it when you bloom
Any moment uncertainty may bring doom
Yet for future there is always hope and room
Don't wait for trouble to come and destroy mood
Today is the best day to drink and eat delicious food.

Gratitude

Gratitude is a good attitude
With ego never substitute
In life you will not face solitude;
Gratitude is thanks giving
Make it your part of living
In life you will be shining;
Gratitude cost you nothing
Yet it can give you many thing
For many relations it is everything;
Be grateful to the helping hand
Positive signal it will send
Forever he will be your friend.

Cost

Unless you control living cost
Under debt you will be lost
Cost always increased by host
Due to high EMI you have to roast
Before spending think for payment most
After wards don't run from pillar to post
Friends will think you to be ghost
Cost can make life from best to worst.

Count

In good days we count up
In bad days starts countdown
In every count the total is determined
Through count profit or loss one can found
Count is always associated with sound
In election count is done in several round
To accept the result everyone is bound
Everything in in life can't be counted by pound.

Best Policy Of Living

Don't measure everything in life by dollar
Better known people are scholar
If you serve people, you can raise collar
Helping mankind also you become taller
Dollar will come and dollar will go
To your goodness nobody will say no
The value of dollar may become low
Yet the value of scholar always grow
Dollar is needed for comfortable living
Best policy is simple living high thinking.

Sun Will Rise Soon

When the spirit is low
When the momentum is slow
When the night is dark
When the street dogs bark
Look to the infinite sky
Give your mind prayer bath
The almighty will show path
The sun will rise very soon
Come out from depressive cocoon.

Single

When you are alone and single
With lot of people you can mingle
You can make friendship triangle
Your relationship you can bundle
Yet your heart and soul never trumble;
If married you face lot of trouble
Many a times you may fumble
But you must have to be humble
Smooth relationships then you can cobble
Otherwise spouse will vanish like bubble.

Birthday

Birthday or date of birth
On this date we came to earth
Balloon, cake and candle
Without wine Birthday can't settle
Important mile stone of journey
Birthday makes joyful our tourney
The celebration was started by other
We have to carry on it further
In the struggle to live poor forget rather.

Counter

Speak or oppose when you are right
Your bouncer may make future bright
If you don't counter journey will be tight
Counter does not mean you have to fight
Your argument may be solid and tight
To counter no need to show your might
Your counter point should not be light
Counter can push truth to greater height.

Country

Demarcation of world made country
It has always a definite boundary
Language and culture binding force
For many people religion is the source
People quarrel for imaginary line
To kill each other for country is fine
People die to keep high country's flag
Battlefields are face of royal stag
Country is the uniting force of human race
Yet for country division people has to face
Olympic represent unity of the countries
Humanity shouldn't encourage boundaries.

Sacrifice

Don't sacrifice animal in the name of God
Animals are God's favourite tiny tod
Never hit animal with your cruelty rod
To sacrifice his kids God will not give nod
Sacrificing animal for God is worst fraud;
Survival of the fittest may be law of nature
Yet God is merciful and take animals care
God eating meat of animal is totally rare
To sacrifice animals in God's name not fair
Jesus sacrificed own life but didn't glare
Sacrifice ego, hatred and your greed
God's love and care animals also need.

Walk

Moving on your own foot
To move forward it is root
Once walking was necessary
In city life it is now luxury
Walking is good for health
It can save money and wealth
Walking helps protecting environment
Walking habit is so very important
Traffic jams walking can reduce
Carbon emission walking don't produce
Walk, walk and burn your excess fat
Environment friendly example you can set.

Water

Another name of water is life
Without it, mankind can't rife
For potable water nature gives rain
Polluting water man always give pain
Unused water flow through the drain
Only through preservation society can gain
In cities water becoming scarce commodity
Yet spoiling water is people's stupidity
Two third of earth is only water
But scarcity of water spreading hunger
Re use of water is now need of the hour.

Umbrella

Black, white, colourful or transparent
The duty of umbrella is always apparent
Appearance of umbrella is not permanent
Not to wet in rain umbrella is supplement
To carry umbrella is not liked by gentlemen;
Umbrella is part of life during rainy season
Many women carry it for fashion reason
During winter umbrella remains in prison
In windy rain umbrella is not a solution
For bike riders rain coat is better evolution.

Coma

Sometimes I wish to go to coma
Will be free from pain and trauma
There will be no profit and loss
Life will continue without any toss
No difference of day and night
No worry for wrong or right
No one will come to make a fight
There will be no more dreaming
Yet time will say that I am living.

Zebra

The indomitable freedom
Never allow to restrict movement
Born free in the wild forever
Taming by human allowed never
Black and white stripes hover
For pedestrian Zebra crossing remember
Zebra is horse's cousin brother
Yet totally different in character.

Zeal

In life don't give up zeal
It makes colourful life's reel
With zeal problems can be peel
Enthusiasm every moment feel
Problems and pain easily heal
Zeal will not allow smile to kill
With zeal succeed in all deal.

Comfort

All struggle in life is for comfort
Hard work needed for its support
For better comfort we need effort
Without work comfort don't report
For earning money comfort don't deport;
Physical comfort money can buy
For greed don't make mental comfort dry
For money don't make health's fry
In search of comfort, you may have to cry.

Comedy

Entertainment to make audience laugh
But for comedian's life is very-very tough
Their day-to-day journey is too rough
Hide tears behind the mask or smile
People's clap inspires to travel many mile
Always on move to make other happy
As if comedians are society's puppy
Our life is not a Shakespeare's comedy
So, for entertainment we need somebody.

Zero

The digit without any value when alone
But when with others it can clone
Zero remains valuable in back foot
In the front foot it has no root
Babylonian, Mayan, Indian used zero first
In modern mathematics zero is must
Hero and zero two sides of the same coin
Someone's victory another's fall zero join
In modern science zero has great significance
In everyday life also zero is equally important.

Commando

Endangering own life for others
Commando always move forward
When police can't control situation
Commando can resolve with intuition
Sophisticated weapons in hand
Commandos are rigorously trained
Commandos protect society from evil
In dealing terrorists, they are daredevil.

Commentator

Commentators are only narrator
They are not society's actual mentor
For money they roam in power corridor
Real problems they rarely monitor;
All commentators are not wise man
Yet they have lot of followers and fan
In search of controversy always ran
Dispute, difference for them golden hen;
However, commentators are needed in society
They should bring people's issues to public politely
Commentators' behaviour should be humility
With people they should always show solidarity.

Citizen, Please Remember

All citizen, please remember
Modi will not be PM forever
He is trying to reform system
To uproot age-old custom
Corruption is in the blood of people
To eradicate it not so simple
Even act can't stop talaq triple
Reform will certainly make ripple
Status quo will make nation cripple
Modified system will bring dimple.

Alcohol

One peg is good
Two pegs smooth
Three pegs loose root
Four pegs unstable foot
Five pegs loud moot
Six pegs throw boot
Little alcohol good for health
In medicine alcohol is wealth
Never become slave of whisky
Life will become hell and risky.

Class

Divide society in the name of wealth and status
If you have money, you are in high class
Without money you are in the mass
Classical music is always classic
Classroom teaches us life's basic
Classmates live in classes society
Classification classified are necessity.

Clean

Free from dirt, marks or pollutant
To clean one's mind is not job instant
To clean society is very difficult
Failure to clean neighbourhood own insult
Clean environment gives good health
Clean nation is every citizen wealth
Cleanliness is next to godliness we say
A clean home always makes beautiful day.

Clap

Clap, clap, clap always clap
But never, never, never slap
You can't clap with one palm
Before you slap try to be calm
Clap is good because it appropriate
Slap is bad because it depreciate
Clap is expression of joy and happiness
Slap is product of anger and mental illness
We pray to God with clap and folded hand
Clap is always spontaneous harmony band.

Deep Corner Of Heart

In the deep corner of heart
Humanity remains always alive
Circumstances make people cruel
For survival happens deadly duel
To become cruel anger add fuel
Those who control anger are jewel
At birth all souls are innocent rural
Yet very few can pass the time's trial.

Move On

When your sky is covered by dark clouds
When thunder gives horrible sounds
Don't stop your steps but move ahead
The rain will come and sky will be clear
The sun will rise again and rainbow there
Don't fear the difficult painful struggling day
After the dark night sun always bring new ray
If you move on boldly time will handsomely pay.

The Show Must Go On

The show must go on
The country must move on
Life may be lost by some son
The country is now in one tone
Planned activities no need to stop
The sinister design of enemy will flop
Together their aggression we will block
Pakistan will reach the bottom rock
It is not the time to weaken government
Every citizen must support with commitment
The show must go on as usual in country
The army is fully capable to protect boundary.

Worst Cruelty

Terrorism is the worst form of cruelty
It throttles and destroys humanity
To fight terrorism, show solidarity
Terrorists are people with doubtful integrity
One religion has given terrorism popularity
Isolate religious terrorists from society
The world is not a place of singularity
Respect religious and ethnic plurality.

Counting

Enjoy the counting of life
Sometimes forward
Sometimes backward
Everyone is busy counting
Someone counting years
Someone months someone days
Sometimes counting money
Sometimes counting debt
But it is never ending race
Yet life is not count of years you live
It is measure of good job you did
Many people died too young
But their legacy forever strong.

Enjoy With Smile

We can't go back
We can only look back
We can't bring back
We can only think back
Don't waste the beautiful moment
Enjoy with smile and good comment
Within a minute it will be past
In the history of time remain as dust
Never allow the present moment to rust
Before time comes, your impression cast
Any moment rainbow bubble may burst.

Citizen

The legal resident of town and country
By birth citizenship has no boundary
Son of the soil is always natural citizen
Though they may be poor artisan
Only citizen have the voting right
Citizen with passport road is bright
Citizen has duties and responsibility
Which they should discharge with solidarity.

Cigarette

Neither a symbol of manhood
Nor cigarette is a good food
The smoke doesn't show aristocracy
Rather its lower spirit of democracy
You have no right to play with others
The smoke destroys health of brothers
Cigarette and tobacco causes cancer
Once infected life will have no answer
Avoid the white tobacco filled cylinder
Many more pages will come in calendar.

Cinderella

The beautiful exploited young girl
The cruel lady abuses every day hurl
Always neglected and ignored by all
Bear everything though she was small
Exploitation of young child not fair
The godmother fairy came to rescue her
In the party she met the charming prince
Finally married her offering weeding ring
For generations the story ignited young mind
In Cinderella plight of child labour we all find.

Cinema

The motion picture that changed entertainment
Rich cousin of theatre art is good enjoyment
Cinema created lot of employment
To industrialisation it is supplement
For mass communication most pertinent
Cinema depicts tragedy and comedy of life
Through cinema a breed of celebrity strive
Charlie Chaplin is loved in all pertinent
Big B Amitabh Bachchan has no retirement.

Circle

Round, round and round
Everywhere circle you found
Circle is a figure bounded by line
With friend circle we are fine
The centre of circle is equidistant
To think out of circle we are hesitant
In life family is the inner circle
For better life family circle never buckle.

Tell Me Your Companion

Tell me your companion, I will tell your character
In the company of horses, donkey also become smarter
Be smart while choosing your friends in life
You will have lot of influences from your wife
The deer can't be friend of a tiger or lion
Any moment the deer can become a pray
A man of straight sex will say no to a gay
If you are not serious while choosing a companion
In the race, you will never become a champion
One day you will become like one of the friends heard
So, listen to your parents and journey with good friends start
Bad friends will pull your legs, so that you can't move up
If you don't accompany to take intoxicant, they will behave rough.

Indian Parents

Indian parents don't encourage children to learn life skills

They are more interested to leave properties through wills

Even at the age of forty, parents are eager to pay children's bills

This way the confidence of their children, they kills

After separation from parents, for them life becomes climbing hills

Parents think, for boys no need to learn cooking and cleaning

Everything their my dear boy will learn from reading

The girls no need to learn driving bikes and vegetables buying

Girls should stay at home after evening, utensils cleaning

Though the mindset is slowly changing in urban areas

Yet, in villages and countryside there are mindset barriers.

Chromosome

Carrier of genetic information
X and Y are its representation
Chromosome is deoxyribonucleic acid
It is necessary for all life's basic
Forty-six chromosomes made human being
The information it carries wonderful thing
Chromosomal aberration cause disorder
In reproduction it remains in the genetic folder
We have no control over our genetic mapping
With good health we can give next-gen a wrapping.

Time Heal Time Kill

Time heals but time also kill
Use of time is the best deal
Utilise your time with zeal
In the world no free meal
Life is recorded in time reel
Time in hand smoothly peel
Don't allow gossip to steal
During sunny day climb hill
Any moment you may be ill
Never accompany rumour mill
Wastage of time will make life nil.

One Night's Guest

In search of nectar
We fly in the morning
Looking flowers at surrounding
Coming and going all are busy
Nobody has time to rest
Before Sunset to collect best
In the evening must return to nest
Our nectar future will taste
In this world we are one night's guest.

Chloroform

The sweet-smelling volatile liquid
For operation theatre important fluid
Chloroform is very good solvent
In laboratory so it is important
Chemistry student use is experiment
When young one can feel its excitement
Sometimes used for kidnapping
For painless surgery chloroform was king.

Chlorophyll

The green blood that produces food
On its shoulder living kingdom stood
Chlorophyll only can do photosynthesis
It is fact and reality not a hypothesis
Chlorophyll is the kitchen of living thing
Without it no animal and birds can sing
Chlorophyll only made the world green
For carbon absorption it is always keen
Trees, plants, grasses are chlorophyll's nest
For survival of mankind planting tree is best.

Beautiful Today

The first glimpses of sun
Remind me it is time to run
The beautiful day brings fun
Yesterday day has gone
Tomorrow may be none
Today's journey must be done;
Today is the most beautiful day
Looking to sunshine I can say
For the wonderful day no need to pay
God has given free rainbow ray
Time will give a new better way
It is my duty to make a good today.

Final Corollary

We are travellers for few days
So, look towards the light rays
Enjoy the beauty even in full moon
You may have to deport very soon;
No need to question why we came
Soon will fade your beauty and fame
Move forward before you are lame
In the graveyard all will be same;
Truth and love are the coronary
Wealth, youth, success all temporary
In the journey only time is contemporary
Graveyard is all traveller's final corollary.

When Jesus In Heart

When Jesus is in heart
You look bold and smart
Big venture you can start
Your mind sin can't dirt
The world is your mart;
When Jesus is in heart
You can carry pain cart
The devil can't hurt
Generosity your chart
Peace become life's part.

Continent

Asia, Africa, America, Australia, Europe
Continents are bonded by humanity rope
In Vatican live our beloved Pope
Jesus's teaching is our only hope
With destructive forces we have to cope;
Continents are only man-made division
Again, there are countries provision
Caste, creed, colour so many emission
Everywhere divisive submission
Love and brotherhood now in omission;
Continent is needed for geography
Division should not be our philosophy
All humans are of the same biology
One world should be mankind's ideology
Jesus gave to humanity best theology.

Longevity Is Not The Yardstick

Butterfly and rainbow don't last long
Yet their presence is very strong
In few minutes ends a melodious song
The longevity is not the true yardstick
If you remain alive lame duck and sick
Make others to smile like butterfly
Your pleasure and joy will touch sky
In the hearts of people rainbow never dry
When you depart with affection people will cry.

Today Is Mine

Dine and wine
Evening is fine
Sit below pine
Near flow Rhine
Look at the vine
Night will shine
Friends will line
Together we will dine
It is already nine
Today is mine.

Confidence

Positive feeling arising from own abilities
Confidence give strength to capabilities
Confidence gives unstoppable progress
Courage and confidence key to success
Confidence motivates to perform better
To achieve goals one can move faster
No confidence push government to fall
Only confidence allow people to stand tall.

About the Author

Devajit Bhuyan

DEVAJIT BHUYAN, Engineer, Advocate, Management & Career Consultant, was born at Tezpur, Assam, India, on 1st August, 1961. He completed Bachelor of Engineering (Electrical), from Assam Engineering College and subsequently completed Diploma in Industrial Management, from International Correspondence School, Mumbai, LL.B. from Gauhati University, Diploma in Management from Indira Gandhi Open University, and Certified Energy Auditor Examination from Bureau of Energy Efficiency (BEE), New Delhi. He is also a Fellow of the Institution of Engineers (India), Life member of Administrative Staff College of India (ASCI) and Assam Sahitya Sabha. He is having 22 years' experience in Petroleum and Natural Gas Sector and 16 years in education management. He has authored 70 books published by different publishers namely, Pustak

Mahal, V&S Publishers, Spectrum Publication, Vishav Publications, Sanjivan Publications, Story Mirror, Ukiyoto Publishing etc. He has also written more than hundred articles in The Assam Tribune, The Northeast Times, The Sentinel, The Oil Field Times, Women's Era, NAFEN Digest, and few other journals. At present, he is the Chairman and Managing Trustee of Mitali Bhuyan Foundation (MBF), and promoting love, brotherhood, peace, tolerance, and nonviolence in society. To know more about him please visit *www.devajitbhuyan.com*

www.ingramcontent.com/pod-product-compliance
Lightning Source LLC
LaVergne TN
LVHW091633070526
838199LV00044B/1046